AFTER-SCHOOL SP⚾RTS CLUB
Time for T-ball

For Mom and Dad
—A. H.

To Mrs. Conolly, Mrs. Karberg,
Mrs. Kimpler, and Mrs. Pearce,
the great first-grade teachers at
Greentree Elementary School!
—S. B.

ALADDIN
An imprint of Simon & Schuster Children's Publishing Division
1230 Avenue of the Americas, New York, NY 10020
First Aladdin paperback edition February 2010
Text copyright © 2010 by Simon & Schuster, Inc.
Illustrations copyright © 2010 by Steve Björkman

For information about special discounts for bulk purchases, please contact
Simon & Schuster Special Sales at 1-866-506-1949 or business@simonandschuster.com.
The Simon & Schuster Speakers Bureau can bring authors to your live event. For more
information or to book an event contact the Simon & Schuster Speakers Bureau at
1-866-248-3049 or visit our website at www.simonspeakers.com.
The text of this book was set in Century Schoolbook BT.
The illustrations for this book were rendered in ink and watercolor.
Manufactured in the United States of America
0610 LAK
2 4 6 8 10 9 7 5 3
Library of Congress Cataloging-in-Publication Data
Heller, Alyson.
Time for t-ball / by Alyson Heller ; illustrated by Steve Bjorkman. — 1st Aladdin pbk. ed.
p. cm. — (After School Sports Club) (Ready-to-read)
Summary: At T-ball practice, Caleb is not very nice when the other children try to hit
the ball, but when it is his turn, he finds that he is not much better.
ISBN 978-1-4169-9412-1 (pbk. edition)
[1. T-ball—Fiction. 2. Sportsmanship—Fiction. 3. Behavior—Fiction.]
I. Bjorkman, Steve, ill. II. Title.
PZ7.H374197Ti 2010   [E]—dc22   2009028109

AFTER-SCHOOL SPORTS CLUB
Time for T-ball

Written by ALYSON HELLER

Illustrated by STEVE BJÖRKMAN

Ready-to-Read

ALADDIN

New York   London   Toronto   Sydney

It was finally spring, and the After-School Sports Club was ready to learn a new sport.

"We are going to try
T-ball," said Mr. Mac.
"Hooray!" said the kids.

Caleb was excited.
"I am gonna hit the ball
on my first try!" he said.

Everyone went to the nearby field and lined up behind the tee.

Alyssa was up first.
She took a swing—
and missed.

"Aw, that was an easy
shot!" said Caleb.

J.B. was up next. He hit
the ball—and knocked
the tee over too!

"J.B., you only hit the ball, not the whole thing!" yelled Caleb.

Mr. Mac frowned.

"Caleb, be nice,"

he said.

"Sorry!" said Caleb.

Sammy and Tess
took their turns.
Sammy lost his bat.

Tess just kept missing.

Finally it was Caleb's turn.

He took a swing—and missed.

"It is okay, Caleb!"
said Alyssa. "Just keep
your eye on the ball!"

Caleb tried again.

And missed.

"Do not worry," said J.B.
"You can do it!"

Caleb felt bad. He had not
been nice to the other kids.
But he could not hit
the ball either!

"Just give it one more try,"
said Mr. Mac.

Caleb took a deep breath.
He swung—and hit the ball
right off the tee.

"Sorry I was mean before,"
said Caleb. "I promise
to be a good sport
from now on!"